CHANGES

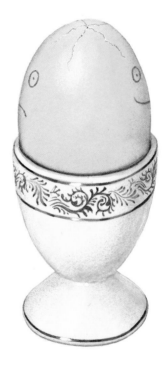

THIS IS A BORZOI BOOK PUBLISHED BY ALFRED A. KNOPF, INC.

Copyright © 1990 by Anthony Browne.
All rights reserved under International and Pan-American Copyright Conventions. Published
in the United States by Alfred A. Knopf, Inc., New York. Distributed by Random House, Inc.,
New York. Originally published in Great Britain by Julia MacRae Books, a division of
Walker Books Ltd., London, in 1990. First American Edition

Manufactured in Hong Kong   2   3   4   5   6   7   8   9   10

Library of Congress Cataloging-in-Publication Data
Browne, Anthony. Changes.
Summary: As he waits at home for his parents to return, a young boy ponders his father's
remark "Things are going to change around here" and begins to imagine all kinds of changes
in the world around him.
[1. Anxiety—Fiction. 2. Imagination—Fiction. 3. Parent and child—Fiction]   I. Title.
PZ7.B81984Ch   1990   [E]   90-4283
ISBN 0-679-81029-3   ISBN 0-679-91029-8 (lib. bdg.)

CHANGES

ANTHONY BROWNE

Alfred A. Knopf 🐎 New York

On Thursday morning
at a quarter past ten,
Joseph Kaye
noticed something strange
about the kettle.

Everything else in the kitchen
was in its familiar place,
clean and tidy.
It even smelled the same as usual.

The house was quiet,
very quiet,
and Joseph's room
was just as he had left it.
And then
he saw the slipper.

That morning, his father had gone
to fetch Joseph's mother.
Before leaving, he'd said
that things were going to change.

Was this what he had meant?

Or this?

Joseph didn't understand.

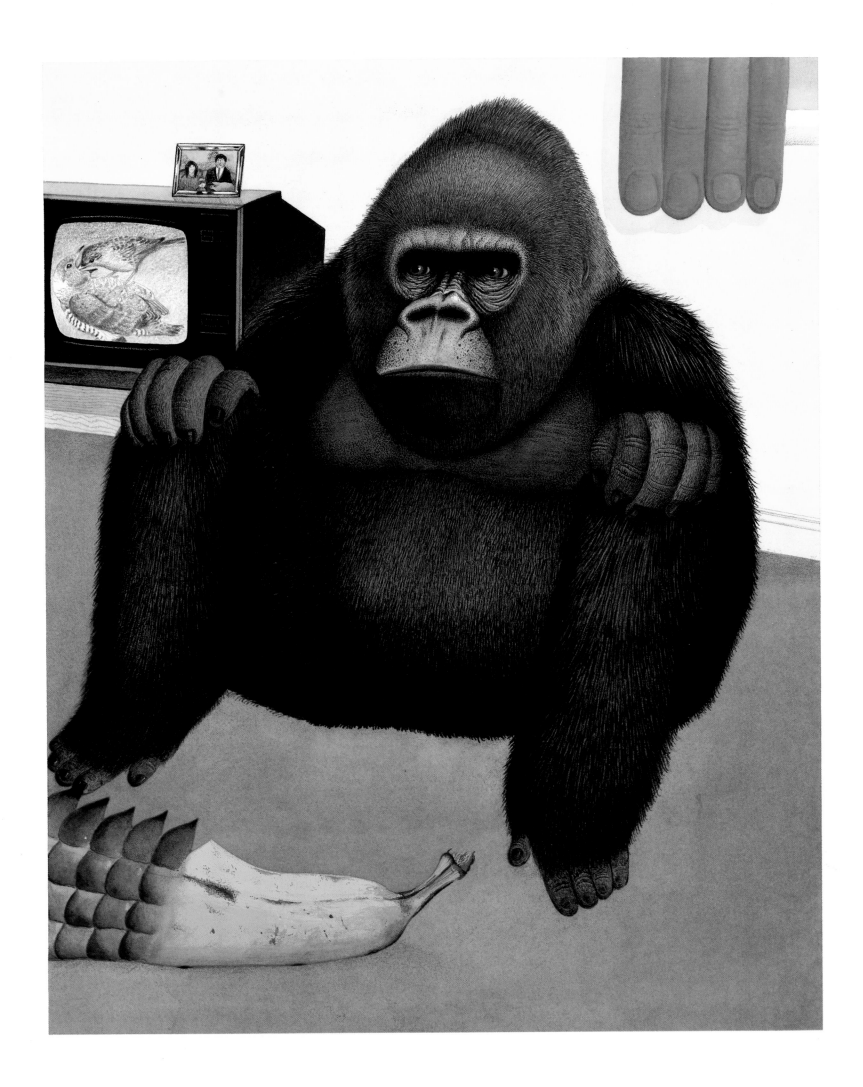

Perhaps things
would be all right outside.
At first they seemed to be.

Joseph didn't know what to do.
Maybe if he went for a ride…

...or looked over the wall?

Was everything
going to change?

Joseph went back
to his room,
closed the door,
and turned off the light.

When the door opened,
light came in,
and Joseph saw
his father,
his mother,
and
a baby.
"Hello, love," said Mom.

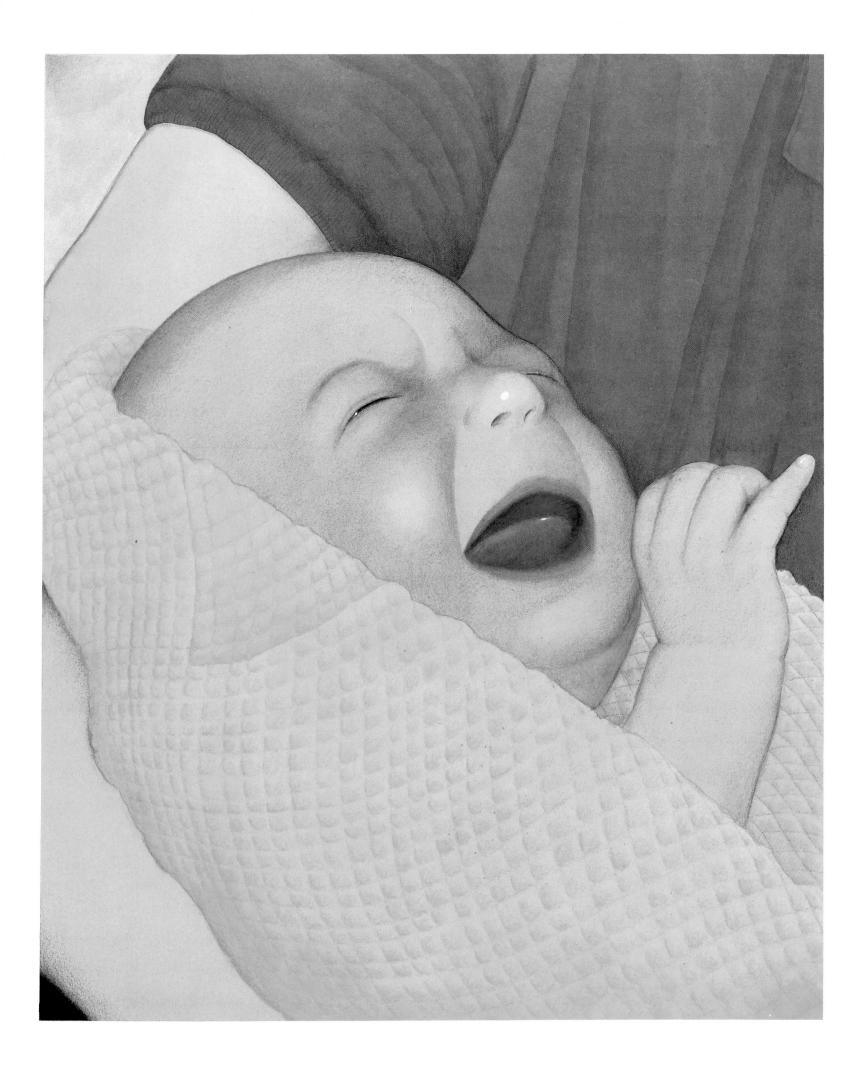

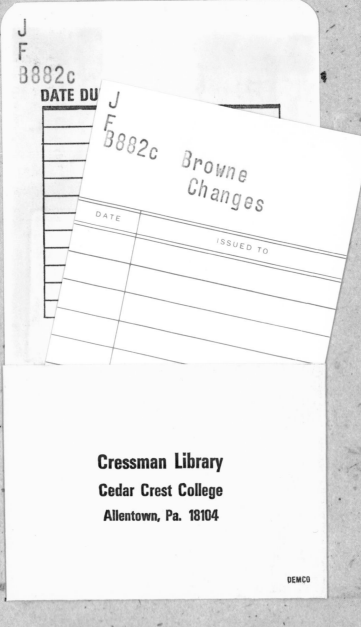